ORCHARD BOOKS
Carmelite House
50 Victoria Embankment
London EC4Y 0DZ

First published in hardback in 2010 by Orchard Books
First published in paperback in 2011

ISBN 978 1 40830 755 7 (HB)
ISBN 978 1 40830 761 8 (PB)

Text © Tony Bradman 2010
Illustrations © Sarah Warburton 2010

A CIP catalogue record for this book is available from the British Library.

1 3 5 7 9 10 8 6 4 2 (HB)
5 7 9 10 8 6 4 (PB)

Printed in Great Britain by CPI Group (UK) Ltd, Croydon CR0 4YY

Orchard Books
An imprint of Hachette Children's Group
Part of The Watts Publishing Group Limited
An Hachette UK Company
www.hachette.co.uk

Tony Bradman

Happy Ever After

THE THREE LITTLE PIGS
GO CAMPING
Illustrated by Sarah Warburton

ORCHARD BOOKS

The Third Little Pig looked at his list and smiled.
He had finished all the tasks he had set himself.
The washing was done… Tick!

The ironing was done… Tick!

The vacuuming...

...and dusting

...and polishing were done... Tick! Tick! Tick!

This was definitely how he liked his life to be. His lovely brick house was nice and tidy, everything organised, sorted, totally under control. Now he could relax, and maybe even watch the new wildlife programme he had read about.

But then again, maybe not. There was always so much that needed to be done! He should spend the evening thinking ahead, and writing up lists of tasks for the next few weeks.

Iron self-discipline was the secret of his success...

Suddenly his mobile rang, almost making him jump out of his skin.

"Hey, big brother!" squeaked the voice on the line. "How are things?"

The Third Little Pig sighed. It was his middle brother, The Second Little Pig. There was a youngest brother as well, The First Little Pig.

The Third Little Pig could hear him squeaking away too, so he knew his brothers were together.

"Er… I can't talk at the moment," said The Third Little Pig. "I'm busy…"

"Writing one of your to-do lists, I'll bet!" squealed The Second Little pig, and laughed.

"Well, I want you to cross out whatever
the first item is and make it this – A Camping
Trip With Your Brothers! Trust me, it's going
to be *fantastic!*"

"Yeah, the best holiday you'll ever have!"
squeaked The First Little Pig.

"I'm sorry, but I really don't think I can fit it in," said The Third Little Pig.

HOUSEHOLD CHORES

CLEAN OUT ATTIC
TIDY GARDEN
DUST SHED
WASH CURTAINS
SEW SOCKS

"Sure I can't tempt you?" said The Second Little Pig. "We've booked a place at Forest Camping Deluxe, so we're going whether you come with us or not…"

The Third Little Pig frowned. He was very fond of his brothers, but they were utterly hopeless in all sorts of ways. In fact, quite often they were real trouble magnets.

Take that unpleasant episode with The Big Bad Wolf, for instance…

In the end they had both come running to The Third Little Pig, and his brick house had kept the wolf at bay.

Not that The First and Second Little Pigs had been terribly grateful. It hadn't been long before they'd moved out again, even though their parents had hired a friendly security guard to look after all of them.

And they would probably get into trouble on this camping trip, thought The Third Little Pig. So he didn't have much choice – he would have to go along to keep them out of trouble.

"All right then, count me in," he said. "But I'll need to do some planning."

"Now there's a surprise," laughed
The Second Little Pig. "You don't have
a lot of time, though, big bro. We'll be
round to pick you up in the morning!"

"*WHAT?*" squealed The Third Little Pig,
horrified. "That's far too soon…"

That evening The Third Little Pig worked hard, doing his packing, reading about the campsite on The Forest Web, making notes (and several new lists)…

He slept badly, and nearly hit the ceiling when his alarm clock woke him.

His brothers were late, and didn't arrive until well after lunch. The Third Little Pig was cross with them, but they weren't bothered. They bundled him and his luggage into their battered old van, and roared off down the road.

"Wow, this is *so* great!" said The First Little Pig when they reached the campsite. "I think there's a river beyond those trees… let's check it out!"

"But… but… what about putting up the tent and getting unpacked?" said The Third Little Pig. "I can't possibly go anywhere till I'm properly settled in!"

"Oh, we can do all that stuff later,"
The First Little Pig said airily.

"Chill out, man," said The Second Little Pig.
"You're on holiday."

"So?" said The Third Little Pig. "What difference does that make?"

"Oh well, suit yourself," said The First Little Pig. "See you later!"

The Third Little Pig watched his brothers scamper away.

A strange feeling passed through him, almost as if he were rather jealous of them...

But then his iron self-discipline kicked in, he gritted his teeth, and he got down to work...

It was quite dark by the time his brothers came back to the tent. They were laughing and chattering, obviously excited.

The Third Little Pig opened his mouth to tell them off for being gone so long, but he never got the chance.

"You should have seen it, big brother!"
said The First Little Pig. "A whole herd of
deer came down to the river...

...and we saw a couple of otters too!"

"That wasn't the best thing though, was it?" said The Second Little Pig. "What about that eagle, then? I never thought I'd see one in The Forest…"

The Third Little Pig definitely felt jealous now. They were so lucky to have seen such things! Thank goodness he had made plans to see some wonderful wildlife himself. Although his plans didn't quite work out as he had hoped…

The next day he wanted to go to a wildlife sanctuary he had read about on The Forest Web. It was the first item on his list, and he couldn't think of doing anything else.

The Second Little Pig, however, didn't seem all that keen.

"But it's really popular," said The Third Little Pig. "Everyone goes there!"

"Exactly," said The Second Little Pig. "I'd rather go somewhere different."

So The Third Little Pig went to the wildlife sanctuary on his own. It turned out to be a major disappointment, with hordes of tourists and not many wild creatures.

OTTER WATERWORLD

GIFTSHOP PLAYGROUND
RABBITS CAFE

And his brothers had much better luck where they had gone.

"You'll never believe what we saw today!" said The Second Little Pig.

The Third Little Pig listened unhappily as his brothers revealed they had stumbled onto a family of beavers that was building a dam...

…and they had seen even more amazing
birds, and then there had been that herd
of wild buffalo…

That evening, The Three Little Pigs sat round their campfire eating a tasty supper. Two of them were cheerful. But one was looking very gloomy indeed.

"Cheer up, big brother!" said The Second Little Pig. "Why the glum face?"

"Yeah, you seem to be having a really bad time," said The First Little Pig.

"I am, and I don't understand it!" squealed
The Third Little Pig. "How come I keep missing
out on seeing all this fantastic wildlife?
What am I doing wrong?"

"Er...maybe you do too much planning," said The First Little Pig. "Of course, it's good to think ahead... But sometimes you should just go with the flow."

"Or do something different," said The Second Little Pig. "It works for me."

It worked for The Third Little Pig as well. The next morning, he got up and looked at his list.

Then he took a deep breath...

...and let his brothers decide what they were all going to do.

And thanks to them, he saw some
amazing things…

A few days later his brothers took
The Third Little Pig back to his lovely
brick house.

He waved happily as they roared off in
their battered old van, and went inside.

Everything was just as he had left it, but there was work to be done.

The Third Little Pig couldn't help himself. He had to sit and write a list. But he added three extra items…

Go with the flow (occasionally);

Do something different (once in a while); and…

Always be sure to have plenty of fun!

So, much to his amazement, The Third
Little Pig managed to live...

HAPPILY EVER AFTER!